Ziggy

The Pig

Who Loved Sushi

Rebecca Mountain-Pazell
Illustrated by Caitlin Bryce Lassen

Outskirts Press, Inc.
http://www.outskirtspress.com

ISBN: 978-1-9772-0849-1

Library of Congress Control Number: 2019907498

PRINTED IN THE UNITED STATES OF AMERICA

For Stella Grace

On a small farm in the state of Kansas, there lived a farmer named John and his wife Veronika. They grew corn and celery and tomatoes and peppers and onions.

They also raised goats and sheep and chickens. But their favorite animal was a small pig named Ziggy. Ziggy was a pink pig with black spots and a long, straight tail. Ziggy had lived with Farmer John and Veronika since she was a few months old. She was given to them as a gift by another farmer.

During the day, Ziggy played in the barn with the other animals, but at night, she went inside the house and ate dinner with Farmer John and Veronika. She liked to curl up in Farmer John's lap when he watched TV. She slept in a little basket on the floor of their bedroom. Ziggy loved being part of their family. Veronika said that Ziggy was a clean, sweet-tempered animal, and so she was pleased to allow a pig inside her home.

One day, Farmer John and Veronika were very excited. "Good news, Ziggy!" they said cheerfully. "Our niece Gina is coming for a visit! She's a student at that big university in Lawrence, Kansas. She's going to stay with us for a few days. Do you promise to be extra-good and not make trouble for Gina when she comes?"

Normally, Ziggy was well-behaved. But, when she smelled tasty food, she sometimes shrieked and screamed until someone gave her a bite. Could she behave during a visit from Gina? Ziggy smiled and wagged her tail happily. She *loved* visitors. She squealed and oinked her way of saying, "Yes, I promise to be good!"

A few days later, Gina drove up to Farmer John's home. He and Veronika ran outside to hug their niece. Ziggy ran outside, too. She couldn't wait to meet Gina. Gina smiled at Ziggy and patted her on the head. Ziggy already knew that she would like Gina as they all walked back into the house.

"Guys, I hope you're hungry," said Gina. "I brought you some sushi from a little Japanese restaurant that I passed on the way to your farm."

"We've never eaten sushi," said Farmer John. "I can't wait to try it and see if it's as delicious as people say it is."

They all gathered around the dining room table. Gina put the sushi pieces on some little plates, and topped them with a dab of something green that she called *wasabi*. She poured a small packet of soy sauce on top of each piece. Then, she took a paper packet of chopsticks and handed them to her aunt and uncle.

"Try it. I think you'll like it. It's a California roll, and has a nice, mild flavor to it."

Uncle John took the first bite, swallowed, and closed his eyes for a moment. "Hey, not bad! Try some, Veronika."

Veronika took a bite and sighed. "Oh, my goodness. Gina, I wish I'd tried this before. It's even better than I hoped it would be."

"If you like that," said Gina, "then try the *enoki* roll. It's made with mushrooms and topped with crispy *tempura* flakes, Japanese mayo, and a sweet and spicy *ponzu* sauce."

Farmer John ate a piece with his fingers and said, "That's even tastier than the California roll! This enoki has a real kick to it!"

All this time, Ziggy was sitting patiently on the floor, watching the family eating the sushi. Ziggy felt hungry, as pigs often do. Earlier that day, as every day, Ziggy enjoyed the meal Veronika prepared for her, which consisted of a special pig feed combined with fresh vegetables and fruits. And on special occasions, Veronika would spoil Ziggy with "people foods," and her favorites were oatmeal, noodles, and sweet desserts. In fact, there weren't any foods that Ziggy disliked, except for pickles and sauerkraut.

But she had never tried sushi before…

The aroma of it was enticing…

Ziggy knew that she had promised to be good and not make any trouble during Gina's visit. But Ziggy really, really wanted to try a piece of sushi. She walked over to Farmer John and shoved her snout into his leg and squealed loudly, as if to say, "Give me a piece of that!"

They all laughed and Veronika said, "Ziggy, we didn't forget about you. I'll let you try a piece to see if you like it."

Veronika put some enoki on a paper napkin and set it on the floor in front of Ziggy. Ziggy sniffed it first, and then carefully snapped it up between her teeth.

WOW! She had never tasted anything so luscious! Sweet, spicy, creamy, crunchy—enoki had all of Ziggy's favorite flavors and textures rolled into one satisfying morsel. Her eyes rolled and her tail wagged vigorously and she oinked loudly to ask for another piece. She wanted to eat an entire roll!

Farmer John said, "Gina, I think you found the way to Ziggy's heart. I don't think she'll ever want to eat anything else!"

Farmer John was right. Ziggy wanted to eat sushi every day. She continued to eat the other foods that Veronika fed her, but she really wanted more sushi.

Gina stayed with her aunt and uncle for a few days, and was sad when her visit came to an end. She gave Ziggy a little hug before she climbed into her car. "Goodbye, Piggy. I'll miss you. I have a friend at school named Mydori. She's from Japan. Japan is the place where sushi was first created. I will tell her all about you and how much you love sushi. I think she will be impressed."

Ziggy was sorry to see Gina leave, but she felt better a few nights later when Farmer John and Veronika went into town for dinner at the Japanese restaurant. "We'll bring you a doggie bag of sushi, Ziggy. We promise."

Ziggy wagged her tail happily. She loved her family. And now, she loved to eat sushi.

"Ziggy, there are going to be some changes, Girl," said Farmer John one day. "Veronika and I are retiring. We found a nice man who will buy our property and take very good care of the animals. We are going to travel around the country in a special camper called an 'RV.' But don't you worry. You're coming with us. We'll travel to interesting places and meet all kinds of people. And yes, we'll stop for sushi in lots of different cities."

Ziggy was upset when she had to say goodbye to the goats and sheep and chickens on the farm. They were her friends. But Farmer John and Veronika promised that she would have exciting adventures once they went out on the road in their RV.

The first day they drove, Ziggy didn't feel good. **At all**. The RV looked comfortable, but once it moved, the ground felt strange underneath her hooves. She had a hard time standing up. And her tummy felt bad in a way it never had before. She heard Veronika tell Farmer John that maybe Ziggy had something called "carsickness." Farmer John stopped driving immediately when he heard this and parked the RV on the side of the road. Veronika gave Ziggy some pink fluid to drink that she said would make Ziggy's tummy feel better. It did. And it was delicious!

After that, Ziggy became accustomed to riding in the RV with Farmer John and Veronika. What fun they had! Ziggy especially loved stopping whenever they found something called "food trucks."

At these food trucks, Veronika allowed Ziggy to sample a variety of satisfying treats. Her favorites were burritos, salads, ice cream cones, and of course, sushi. Ziggy even tried exciting new styles of sushi in different American cities. Kansas City-style sushi, St. Louis-style, Chicago-style, Philadelphia-style… she loved them all, and she learned to eat sushi from the chopsticks that Veronika held for her!

She also appreciated the attention that people paid to her whenever they saw her devouring sushi rolls at the many food trucks they visited. Countless people took her picture and shot little videos of her and said that they would put it on social media.

A TV news station in Dubuque, Iowa even featured Ziggy on a local broadcast. Ziggy was attracting so much attention now that Farmer John had to make sure that Ziggy wore her harness and her leash at every food stop. "I don't ever want you to run away and get lost, Girl. Especially now that you're famous!"

"Oh, John, stop. Ziggy isn't actually famous," laughed Veronika.

"Sure she is," he responded. "Gina said that those pictures of Ziggy eating sushi have gone viral. Now, thousands of people have heard of her and want to take selfies with her!" Farmer John was right. Many people knew about Ziggy, the pig who traveled cross-country, eating sushi in numerous cities. But Ziggy's popularity wasn't limited to the United States. Gina called to tell Uncle John and Aunt Veronika some marvelous news—Ziggy was a global sensation! She was being followed on social media by fans all over the world. Mydori, Gina's college friend in Lawrence, had liked the photos and videos of Ziggy eating sushi so much that she shared the pictures with her family back in her hometown of Hiratsuka, Japan. And those images became popular there much as they had in the United States and the rest of the world. Hiratsuka and Lawrence, KS are sister cities, and Mydori's cousin worked for the mayor of Hiratsuka. So now, the mayor of Hiratsuka wanted Farmer John and Veronika to fly to Japan and to bring Ziggy! They would be guests in a special ceremony as an act of goodwill between the two cities.

⟵

"Ziggy, promise you'll go to sleep as soon as the plane takes off," said Veronika as she tucked Ziggy securely inside her travel cage. "It is a very long flight."

Indeed, the flight from Los Angeles, CA to Tokyo, Japan was long. Ziggy's head was swimming with thoughts of all kinds. The lengthy examination the veterinarian performed on Ziggy before she could leave the country. The photographers who took her picture before she boarded the plane…the friendly people who all smiled and petted her and told her that now they wanted to buy a pig because they had enjoyed the social media photos and videos of her being fed sushi with chopsticks. Ziggy was excited with all of this newfound attention…but she still missed her animal friends on the farm.

She thought about them every single day.

The plane landed very late in the evening in Tokyo.

Ziggy felt itchy and her mouth was dry from the long flight. Farmer John gave Ziggy something to drink to help her feel better, and she did.

The three of them were now in Japan--time for the adventure to begin!

A taxicab took them from the airport to a special hotel that allowed animals to stay in the same room as their humans. A smiling employee at the hotel told Ziggy that she was the first pig to spend a night there.

Ziggy and Farmer John and Veronika all slept on a *tatami* mat on the floor. It was soft and comfortable. Ziggy loved snuggling close with them. It reminded her of napping next to the sheep back on the farm in Kansas.

The next day, another taxi came to drive them from Tokyo to Hiratsuka. Ziggy was wearing a brand-new harness as she climbed in the cab. Veronika had wiped her clean that morning and told her that she needed to look her best for the ceremony that day.

Ziggy loved this car trip through Japan! She saw cherry blossom trees for miles.

And breathtaking gardens! Veronika gasped and said, "I think Japan is the most gorgeous place I've ever seen!"

And lots of people! They didn't ever remember seeing so many people in one place. Farmer John and Veronika noticed that many people were dressed in suits and ties…but some were wearing flowered kimonos.

Some *Harajuku* teenagers had on colorful wigs and flamboyant clothing unlike anything they saw back home in Kansas.

After riding for about two hours, Farmer John said, "We're here. Ziggy, remember that you have to be good. You're going to meet the mayor!" Veronika held Ziggy's leash nervously as they stepped out of the taxicab. A very pretty woman came forward and said "*Konicheewa*. My name is Sachiko, and I will be your interpreter. The mayor is ready to meet you now. We are having your welcoming ceremony here in the garden."

The garden contained well-manicured cherry trees and festive lanterns. Ziggy noticed a large group of people standing in the distance. Many were holding cameras. A journalist was speaking into a microphone while he was being videotaped. As Sachiko led them toward the newsman, Veronika whispered to Farmer John, "This is the most thrilling moment of our lives!" He agreed. "I know! I cannot believe that this whole celebration is just for us and our little pig—and to think that all this started because Gina introduced Ziggy to sushi!"

Farmer John saw several long tables covered in white cloths that had beautiful flowers, fruit baskets, and large platters of sushi.

These were the most elaborate sushi rolls that Veronika had ever seen. But that wasn't what attracted Ziggy's attention. She saw something else. And she had to run toward it!

OINK! SQUEAL! ZIGGY TORE OFF IN A MAD DASH! Veronika lost her grip on the leash. Ziggy ran away so forcefully that she knocked over several folding chairs and a potted plant! What a loud commotion! She squealed and kept running and ignored Farmer John's commands. "Ziggy, stop that! Come back here this minute!"

Farmer John saw the mess that Ziggy made, then bit his lower lip and shook his head in embarrassment. Veronika looked horrified and said tearfully to Sachiko, "We are terribly sorry that Ziggy is misbehaving this way. Please apologize to the mayor for us."

But Sachiko didn't seem to hear. Instead, she pointed at something in the distance and said, "Look. Look at your pig." Farmer John and Veronika saw a little girl in a pink-and-red kimono. She was smiling and holding a leash. At the end of the leash was a small brown pig, who looked much like Ziggy, except that he had little tusks.

The little girl said something that Sachiko translated to Farmer John in English.

"His name is *Danshi*. That means 'Big Boy' in Japanese. This little girl says that he likes to eat sushi, just like your Ziggy. She shows him photos and videos of your Ziggy, and Danshi enjoys them very much."

Ziggy walked to Danshi and nuzzled him gently. He rubbed his snout over hers, as if to say "Let's be friends."

"Well, I don't think the pigs need an interpreter, do they, Sachiko?" asked Farmer John, while Veronika laughed.

"No, Mister John, they seem to communicate very well."

"I guess I never realized how much my famous little pig missed her animal friends on the farm," said Farmer John a bit sheepishly.

Veronika agreed, "I suppose that Ziggy loves companionship, even more than she loves eating sushi."

While the photographers were busy taking pictures of the snuggling pigs, the mayor came over to greet Farmer John and Veronika. The mayor smiled warmly and bowed.

"Mr. Mayor, we can't thank you and the people of Japan enough for your graciousness and hospitality," said Farmer John. He presented the mayor with a gift bag of souvenirs from home, including a packet of seeds to plant sunflowers. Veronika asked Sachiko to tell the mayor that not only are sunflowers the official flower of Kansas, but they also symbolize unity, loyalty, and good health. The mayor beamed and expressed that he was honored to have them as guests.

The man with the microphone asked Farmer John if he would like to say something to the TV news camera. "Yes, I realized today that animals are much like people, even more than I had ever thought. We all want the same things—comfort, good food, but most of all, friendship," he said.

Just then Ziggy pushed Farmer John's leg with her snout and squealed.

"Yes, Ziggy," he said. "I wish that we could stay here, too. But we have to go home soon. Back to Kansas. We'll buy a small place with a yard. And get another pig for you, Ziggy. And after what I saw today, I know that we'll stay there for a long, long time."

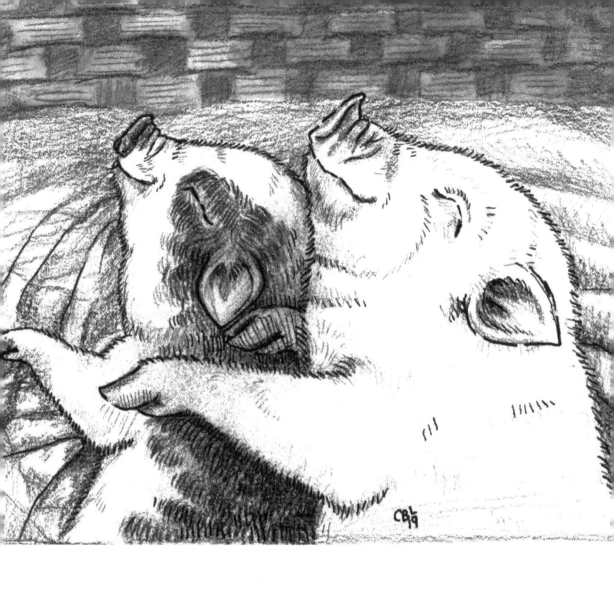

And they did…

...happily ever after.

~The end.